Alexis and

Jan,

Santa's Our
Substitute Teacher!

Watch out for the

Hoooosh Kas !

Kevin Kremer

Other books
by Kevin Kremer:

A Kremer Christmas Miracle

Spaceship Over North Dakota

Saved by Custer's Ghost

The Blizzard of the Millennium

When it Snows in Sarasota

Santa's Our Substitute Teacher!

by Kevin Kremer

Illustrated by Dave Ely

Published by Snow in Sarasota Publishing
2006
P.O. Box 1360
Osprey, FL 34229-1360
www.snowinsarasota.com

First printing, 2006
Copyright © 2006 Snow in Sarasota Publishing
P.O. Box 1360
Osprey, FL 34229-1360
www.snowinsarasota.com

ISBN 0-9663335-4-3

Printed in the United States of America

This book is dedicated to the remarkable people from Mandan, North Dakota — my hometown.

1

'Twas a few nights before Christmas—the night of December 20th to be exact—definitely crunch time for everyone at the North Pole.

Santa scheduled a meeting with his team leaders in the Conference Room at Santa's Toy Factory for nine o'clock that night. Santa, Mrs. Claus, and Santa's chief of staff, Ziggy, showed up early for the meeting. Also in attendance were the twelve elves who were the team leaders at the North Pole: Kristin, Patricia, Shaquira, Makala, Kelly, Mikey, Maynard, Willzer, Jared, Marcos, Sheldon, and Charlie.

Everyone sat comfortably around an enormous, red, round table—eating cookies, talking, and drinking hot chocolate. Santa swallowed the last bite of a delicious reindeer cutout cookie, then he cleared his throat to get everyone's attention.

"I know how extremely tired and busy all of you must be," said Santa, "so we'll make this quick. Let me turn the meeting over to Ziggy at this point."

Ziggy, who was sitting on Santa's right, was a very smart, no-nonsense elf with a long white beard. His face reminded everyone of Ben Franklin.

He stood up with a green clipboard in his right hand and spoke in a deep voice, pronouncing each word carefully. "A couple of things have come up that I felt we must discuss immediately. Kristin will share the first matter with us."

Ziggy returned to his seat. Kristin, the leader of the Letters to Santa Team, was sitting directly across the table from Santa and Mrs. Claus. Except for her distinctly elfin ears, Kristin looked like she might have been a typical third grader. In reality, though, she was actually a mature elf—just over 953 years old.

Kristin stood up, holding a large photograph up in the air for everyone to see. The photo showed Kristin sitting at her desk in her office. Several huge stacks of letters were piled up on her desk, and five bags full of letters were lying on the floor nearby.

Kristin spoke in her childlike voice. "We took this photo down in my office just before I came to this meeting," she said. "Does anyone want to guess what all the letters in this picture have in common?"

Charlie, the fun-loving leader of Santa's Sleigh Maintenance Team, who was sitting three seats to the left of Kristin, smiled and said, "They wouldn't all be your love letters, would they?"

There were many giggles from around the table. Kristin made a face at Charlie. "Sorry, Charlie. Not even close. Actually, all of these letters and millions more were written by good boys or girls who just happen to have the same item at the

top of their Santa Wish Lists this year ... something that unfortunately none of us at the North Pole can make for them."

Patricia, the leader of the Reindeer Grooming Team, asked, "What are they asking for, Super Bowl Tickets?"

"Good try," Kristin replied, biting her lip, trying hard to remain serious. "Every single boy or girl wants the same thing—a white Christmas this year. Isn't there *anything* we can do about this?"

Mikey, team leader of Research and Development, spoke up. "Look, we've been working on this white Christmas problem for hundreds of years, Kristin. I think we've made some progress ... in fact, one of my brightest scientists is actually testing a prototype, but I don't think his early trials have been too promising."

"Who's this scientist you're talking about, Mikey?" Mrs. Claus wanted to know.

"Patrick," Mikey answered.

Patrick was known to be extremely smart and creative, yet very jittery and more than a little scatterbrained. He often had difficulty finishing projects once he got started working on them.

"Oh, yes … Patrick," Santa said thoughtfully. After thinking for a few seconds, Santa added, "If you don't mind, I'd like to talk to Patrick right now and get a firsthand status report on his work."

"I'll bet he's in our lab," Mikey guessed. "Try there first."

In a few seconds, Patrick appeared on the huge TV screen in the Conference Room. He was sitting in the laboratory, surrounded by unfinished projects, his nose buried in a book.

"Hello, Patrick. This is Santa."

Patrick was so startled he dropped his book and nearly fell out of his chair!

"Oh! Oh, h-h-hi, Santa," he said, trying to settle himself down. "Sorry … you startled me a little."

"I apologize for that, Patrick," said Santa. "We're having a meeting of team leaders over here, and Mikey's been telling us about a snowmaking device you've been working on for awhile. Could you please tell us a little bit about it?"

"Oh, s-sure," Patrick replied. "Well ... I'm working on a small device I call the SN-1224 that can be attached to the back of your sleigh ... It-it's over in another room some place—I could get it and show you."

"No, that's all right, Patrick," Santa said. "Just describe it to us if you can."

"Well, I'm trying to make it aerodynamic—so it won't slow down your sleigh and reindeer significantly ... the SN-1224 would theoretically draw moisture out of the air, store it, and convert it into crystals ... the crystals would eventually become big, beautiful snowflakes. I was hoping to formulate snowflakes that would fall all the way to the ground—even in the warmest parts of the world— maybe even come up with special snowflakes that would stay on the ground awhile before they melted—so everyone in the world could have a white Christmas, at least for an hour or two."

"Sounds quite impressive," Santa observed. "How have your early tests gone?"

"S-s-so many problems—so many problems," Patrick replied nervously.

"I was just wondering," said Santa, bracing himself for Patrick's reaction. "What would it take to have your device ready by Christmas Eve?"

"This year!" Patrick exclaimed, almost flying out of his chair. "That's impossible, Santa! S-so many problems—so little time."

"Look, Patrick," Santa said calmly. "I want you to focus on this snowmaking thing the next few days and see how far you can get with it. I'll have Mikey get all the other brain power on your Research and Development Team to help you as much as possible. See what you can do."

"S-Santa?" said Patrick, trying to regain his composure.

"Yes, Patrick."

"I would need to do some testing outside the lab with your sleigh and reindeer—and I know how you like to keep the reindeer rested before their big night on Christmas Eve."

"Don't worry about the reindeer," Santa said. "Rudolph and the rest of the reindeer still need a few hours of exercise each day no matter what. They can even handle a bit more than that if need be. Patrick, you just try your best to get that snowmaking machine of yours ready by Christmas Eve. We have so many good girls and boys asking for a white Christmas. I hate to disappoint all of them."

"OK, Santa," Patrick said, "but I hope you're not t-too upset if we don't finish this thing for another year or two."

"I could never be upset with you, Patrick," said Santa. "Just do your best and please keep me informed."

"OK, Santa. I will."

"I won't keep you any longer then, Patrick. Good-bye."

"Bye, Santa."

Patrick disappeared from the large screen, and Santa said, "What's next, Ziggy?"

"Maynard has something for us," Ziggy stated.

The head of the Last Minute Santa Letters Team, a spunky young elf named Maynard, stood up, holding a letter in his hand. For the first time in a long time, Maynard didn't have a big smile on his face. In fact, he looked very sad, about ready to cry.

"What's wrong, Maynard?" Santa asked in a concerned voice.

"We've got an extremely sad letter that just arrived here an hour ago," Maynard answered. "It's from Miss Kemper, a fourth grade teacher from Mandan, North Dakota, USA. Many of you remember her as *Medora* Kemper."

All of the elves around the table nodded their heads and smiled.

"Yes, yes," said Santa. "She's been such a good person her whole life. Please read Medora's letter."

"All right," Maynard said. "Here goes ... but you'd better get your Kleenex ready."

Dear Santa,

I'm sorry for bothering you at such a busy time of the year, but I thought you might be able to help me. As you know, my fourth graders and I have always loved Christmas. It's always been our favorite time of the year.

This year, however, has been different. I'm having a rather difficult year, and I'm afraid my

11

fourth graders and I don't seem to have much Christmas spirit at all.

Now, I'm very sad, because it's the last week of school before Christmas. Unfortunately, I have to go into the hospital for surgery tomorrow, so I don't have any more time to try to get some Christmas spirit going in my classroom.

If there's anything you can do to help me, please do.

Love,
Medora Kemper

Tears had formed in everyone's eyes. Some elves started crying out loud.

"Oh, my. That's so sad," Patricia said, tears flowing down her cheeks.

"We've got to do something," Kristin said, sniffling.

"What can we possibly do?" Ziggy asked.

"I know *exactly* what to do!" Santa said with a determined look on his face. "I'll go to Mandan and be Medora's substitute teacher for these few days before Christmas vacation. It sounds to me like we've got things pretty much under control here at the North Pole anyway. Besides, if something comes up, you can easily get in touch with me in Mandan."

Mrs. Claus looked over at Santa with a shocked expression on her face. "And what do *you* know about teaching?" she asked, speaking much louder than usual.

Santa looked a little offended. "Honey, I may know almost nothing about teaching, but I know more about children than almost anyone."

Mrs. Claus was blunt. "I love you, Dear—but those fourth graders would eat you alive."

Santa thought hard about a response. Then he spotted Willzer across the table and got a brilliant idea.

"Look, if it will make you feel any better, I'll take Willzer along with me," Santa said.

Willzer nodded and smiled approvingly. Willzer was only nine and a half inches tall, and he had the face of a first grader. In fact, he was over 519 years old and the most experienced teacher at North Pole Elementary School.

Mrs. Claus thought this over briefly. "With Willzer's help, maybe you could make it through a few days of teaching," she said, feeling much better about the situation.

"Ziggy?" said Santa. "Do you think all the details could be worked out?"

Ziggy looked confident. "It may take more than a little magic," he said, "but you've given me even tougher challenges in the past."

2

The North Pole—December 21st— 5:00 A.M. Only three days left till Christmas Eve.

Santa's sleigh and reindeer were being readied for flight in a large snow covered clearing in the back of Santa's house. Three elves named Dave, Jenny, and Cindy were pouring over every inch of the sleigh. They were checking and double-checking each detail to ensure a safe flight. Three other elves were feeding and pampering the reindeer, who all seemed anxious to fly again. Four more elves were loading the sleigh with trunks, suitcases, reindeer treats, and other supplies.

Another elf was sitting in Santa's seat on the sleigh, making sure all aeronautical systems were operational. This was Ethan, the North Pole's young hotshot test pilot. Although Ethan was a gifted flyer, Santa often had to remind him not to act like such a daredevil. After all, Santa's sleigh was not really built for stunt flying.

Santa, Mrs. Claus, Willzer, and Patrick walked out of Santa's house toward the sleigh. Mrs. Claus, who was still a little worried about the whole substitute teaching situation, was looking for some last minute reassurance.

"Willzer," she said, "will you please make sure Santa doesn't make a fool of himself with those fourth graders?"

"Don't worry," Willzer replied. "I'll be nearby in the classroom at all times. Santa and I are both going to have fun the next few days."

Mrs. Claus smiled just slightly. "I hope so, Willzer. Just do me a big favor—keep in touch so I don't have to sit back here at the North Pole worrying about what's happening all the time."

As they approached the sleigh, Santa said, "Willzer and I will keep you informed, Dear—and I would appreciate it if you would keep things under control at the North Pole in my absence."

"I will," said Mrs. Claus.

As Santa's reindeer watched, Santa gave Mrs. Claus a good-bye kiss. The reindeer started making some funny reindeer sounds, teasing Santa and Mrs. Claus a little. Mrs. Claus thought she heard Dasher say *smoochy smoochy*—then all the reindeer laughed.

Santa, Willzer, and Patrick boarded the sleigh. Santa's meteorologist, an ancient-looking elf with a long gray beard named Dewey, approached the sleigh and gave Santa the latest weather conditions.

Dewey spoke in a hoarse, yet friendly voice. "Except for a few snow flurries near the United States-Canadian border, this is a spectacular morning for flying," Dewey began. "The skies will be clear with plenty of moonlight all the way to North Dakota. No wind to speak of. The temperature this morning is a pleasantly nippy twenty-one below Fahrenheit here at the North Pole, and it should warm up to a blazing ten below zero by the time you get to Mandan." Dewey tried to laugh at his last remark, but he croaked out a cough instead.

Santa looked at his wife with a big smile and said, "Ho! Ho! Ho! Ten below! I hope you packed my red Bermuda shorts, Dear."

Everyone had a good laugh as Santa, Patrick, and Willzer got on board the sleigh. Ethan slid over to the seat next to Santa. Patrick and Willzer got settled in some seats behind them.

After they'd fastened their safety belts, Santa yelled:

"All right, Dasher and Rudolph,
     Dancer, Prancer, and Vixen!
   Now, Comet and Cupid,
     And Donner and Blitzen!
   Let's fly directly to Mandan,
     Willzer and I are teaching today!
   Miss Kemper needs a substitute,
     Now, let's be on our way!"

Everybody on board the sleigh and on the ground waved as the sleigh took off slowly, gained altitude gradually, then climbed rapidly high into the moonlit sky and headed south.

On Christmas Eve, this flight to North Dakota would take less than ten minutes because the reindeer would be allowed to fly at top speed. On this particular morning, however, Santa wanted his nine reindeer to conserve their energy for the big night to come. Consequently, total flight time this morning would be close to an hour. The extra time would give Santa, Willzer, Ethan, and Patrick a last chance to talk about some of the challenges that lie ahead for them.

In a few minutes they were flying near Yellowknife, Canada. Santa's reindeer were thrilled to see large herds of their friends and relatives down below.

Santa called out to his reindeer, "Let's drop down and buzz your friends! After that, we'll take the scenic route to Mandan this beautiful morning! Let's fly over Lake Louise and Calgary, then past the North Dakota State Capitol before we land in Mandan ...

Did you get all that, Rudolph?"

Rudolph looked back at Santa, then snorted a little as if he were slightly insulted. *Of course, he got it.*

The rest of the reindeer roared excitedly. They were extremely pleased with the flight plan.

The next instant, the reindeer and sleigh made a roller-coaster dive that thrilled Ethan, but almost brought Patrick and Willzer's stomachs right up into their throats. Seconds later, they leveled out at a low altitude and slowly flew over hundreds of reindeer grazing down below.

Ethan looked over at Santa, smiled, and said, "Who's the daredevil, Santa?" Santa gave Ethan a playful, mischievous smile back.

The reindeer on the ground looked up in the air and exchanged lots of friendly messages with their lucky flying reindeer friends. Then Patrick and Willzer pushed a huge bag of special treats out the back of the sleigh and watched as the bag slowly parachuted to the ground below.

"It's an early Christmas present from all of us!" Santa yelled down to the reindeer. "Ho! Ho! Ho! Merry Christmas!"

The reindeer on the ground looked up in the air and roared, bawled, and grunted loudly to show their thanks as Santa's sleigh and reindeer flew toward Edmonton. Along the way, Ziggy contacted the sleigh from his office at the North Pole. His face appeared on the small TV screen in front of the sleigh as he spoke.

"Let's go over some of the details of your little teaching adventure," Ziggy said. "When you get to Mandan, you'll be staying at the Lewis and Clark Hotel on Main Street."

"Oh, good," said Santa cheerfully. "I know it well. A wonderful place."

"Yes, it is," said Ziggy. "As you know, Santa, the hotel has a large flat roof, so you should be able to make an easy, inconspicuous landing in the dark when you get there this morning. There's a comfortable suite on the top floor called the Presidential Suite. Teddy Roosevelt actually stayed there once—you're already checked in. You'll actually be able to access your suite right from the roof. Once you've unloaded everything from the sleigh, Ethan will pilot the sleigh back to the North Pole. Patrick, on the return trip this morning, you can talk to Ethan about your likely schedule for testing that snowmaking device of yours. Ethan, I want you available for Patrick's tests whenever he needs you."

Santa glanced in his rearview mirror and noticed that Patrick was looking worried. "Don't worry about anything, Patrick," Santa said. "Let's just do everything we can to try to get your snowmaking device ready by Christmas Eve. If we don't make it this year, we'll try hard for next year."

"Sounds good," Patrick said, looking a little less anxious but still feeling the pressure.

Ziggy continued his run-through. "Santa and Willzer—from the hotel, it's a short walk to Jim Coats Elementary School where you'll be substitute teaching."

"I know exactly where that is," said Santa.

Ziggy added, "The kids in Mandan get out of school on December 23rd at noon, so you've got less than three teaching days to get through. While you're substituting, Santa, you'll be *Mr. Clausnitzer*. Willzer, there's a special red trunk we've loaded on board the sleigh. You'll be able to hide in it and communicate with Santa if he needs any help with his teaching. You two will have to find the best place to put the trunk in the classroom sometime this morning before school starts."

"Sounds good," Willzer said.

"Ziggy?" asked Santa. "Was it difficult for you to arrange for me to be the substitute teacher?"

"Not really," Ziggy replied. "To be honest, the principal seemed relieved to find any substitute at all. He thought *he* was going to have to teach the class until Christmas vacation, and I got the feeling he dreaded that possibility."

"I wonder why he had problems finding a substitute," said Willzer.

"Maybe 'cause it's such a busy time of the year for everyone," Santa suggested.

"I hope that's it," Willzer said. "I wish I wasn't getting the strange feeling Miss Kemper's class may be more of a challenge than we think."

24

Ziggy hesitated. "Uh … actually … I'm afraid you may be right about that, Willzer."

"What do you mean?" Willzer wanted to know.

"Well … I don't want to alarm you," Ziggy began uneasily, "but our Naughty and Nice Research Department did a quick analysis of the kids on Miss Kemper's class list. There seems to be a set of triplets in the class that could be the potential source of some trouble … Brian, Braydon, and Tyler Hooooshka—the last name is oddly spelled with four consecutive O's."

"Strange," Santa observed. "I don't believe I've ever seen four consecutive O's in *any* name before."

"Nor had anyone in our Naughty and Nice Research Department," said Ziggy. "They also couldn't find much information about these Hooooshka triplets. They've never believed in you, Santa, so they're not even in our Christmas database. From what we were able to dig up, the Hooooshkas showed up at Jim Coats Elementary on Halloween from somewhere near Blackfoot, Idaho. To put it kindly, they've caused some huge problems at the school ever since."

"What kind of problems?" Willzer asked.

"We don't have a lot of details yet, but we know Miss Kemper is one of the best teachers anywhere, and she's had an awful time since the Hooooshkas showed up. She had one substitute teacher in November when she was attending a workshop. Rumor has it—that guy left the school before noon crying because of something the Hooooshkas did."

"Do you have any pictures of the Hooooshka boys?" Santa asked.

"Yes, we do," Ziggy replied, cringing. "I'll transfer them to your screen."

"Yikes!" Willzer exclaimed when the boys' pictures appeared on the screen. "Those boys look like seventh or eighth graders!"

"Oh, m-m-my," Patrick stuttered. "I've seen mug shots of criminals that looked more pleasant."

Ethan giggled. "Those guys need more than a substitute teacher. I suggest you call the United States Marines," he said.

"What about the boys' parents?" asked Santa.

"That's a mystery to us so far," Ziggy answered.

"We're pretty sure the parents dropped Brian, Braydon, and Tyler off at the school in Mandan on Halloween, but that's the last evidence we have of them. There are some more rumors that the Hooooshka triplets are now living all by themselves in an old rundown farmhouse north of Mandan."

Willzer looked uneasy. "Santa, we may be getting into more of a challenge than we can handle here. No wonder Miss Kemper is having such a tough time getting the class in the Christmas spirit. Maybe we should turn the sleigh around and head back to the North Pole."

"Nonsense," said Santa. "You and I can handle this, Willzer. Besides, we owe it to Miss Kemper to give it our best effort."

Willzer said, "OK, but I just want you to know this substitute teaching assignment isn't going to be easy, Santa."

"Don't worry, Willzer," Santa said. "We can do it."

Soon they were flying over the snow-frosted Rocky Mountains southwest of Edmonton and the gigantic hotel called the Fairmont Chateau Lake

Louise, which was lit up with thousands and thousands of extra lights for the Christmas season.

Santa said, "This is Mrs. Claus's second favorite vacation place in the whole world. From the window of our hotel room we can see that majestic glacier over there, the spectacular lake, the awesome Rocky Mountains, and all those beautiful trees. It's truly breathtaking."

"It sure is, Santa," Patrick agreed. "If this is Mrs. Claus's second favorite vacation spot, her favorite place must be incredible. Where is that?"

"Siesta Key Beach on the Gulf Coast of Florida," Santa replied. "I think she especially enjoys the warmer weather there a few weeks each winter— and the beach's sand is almost as white as snow and as soft as powdered sugar."

Ten minutes later, they got to Bismarck, and they flew near North Dakota's State Capitol Building.

"Look!" Ethan yelled, pointing at the nineteen-story building.

The custodians had turned on the lights in selected offices especially for the Christmas

season. The pattern of the lights formed a huge likeness of Santa on one side of the tall building.

"The custodians have been doing this every Christmas season since the 1930's," said Santa. "Let's fly closer and see if we can give the custodians a big thank-you."

Santa guided the sleigh within twenty yards of the building, flying past the windows a few times, trying to get someone's attention. Finally, two very surprised custodians opened up a window on the fourteenth floor, stuck their heads out, and yelled, "Hi, Santa!"

"Ho! Ho! Ho! Thanks for the nice tribute!" Santa yelled back. "I'll see you again in a few days!"

"You're welcome, Santa! Bye!" one of the custodians yelled back as the sleigh and reindeer flew toward Mandan.

From the State Capitol Building, it was less than a minute flying time to the Lewis and Clark Hotel in nearby Mandan. When Santa's sleigh landed on the roof of the hotel in the dark, no one in Mandan even noticed—but dogs all over town started barking.

3

After the four of them unloaded the sleigh, Ethan and Patrick got right back on board, ready to fly back to the North Pole.

Just before they took off, Santa said, "Patrick, don't forget to keep me informed ... and Ethan, please fly safely."

"Good luck with everything, Ethan and Patrick," Willzer added. "Patrick, I hope you get your contraption ready by Christmas Eve."

"I think Santa and you might need more luck than Ethan and I do," Patrick observed. "Compared to what you two have to do the next few days, I suddenly don't feel so nervous about the SN-1224 anymore."

"We'll be just fine," Santa said confidently. Then Santa called out to his reindeer, "Now, take them home, my phenomenal reindeer!" The sleigh and reindeer slowly lifted off the roof, then accelerated rapidly into the darkened sky.

Mayor Bob Dykshoorn, who was taking his morning stroll along Mandan's Main Street, was deep in thought as the sleigh whooshed above his head at high speed. He quickly looked up into the air and thought he saw a falling star—only it wasn't falling. Instead, it was going up into the sky like a multicolored supersonic bottle rocket.

"Maybe I've been working too many hours," the mayor said out loud to himself.

Santa and Willzer went to the Presidential Suite to get ready for school. As soon as they got there, Santa called George's Bakery in Mandan, one of his favorite bakeries in the whole world.

"Hello, this is ... uh, Mr. Clausnitzer ... in the Presidential Suite at the Lewis and Clark Hotel. Do

you think you could have someone deliver a dozen of your most delicious chocolate iced donuts to my room as soon as possible? ... Oh, thank-you ... Bye."

The donuts were delivered in less than ten minutes. As Willzer started eating donuts and drinking coffee, Santa changed into a very stylish dark green suit, a red and white striped tie, and black casual shoes. The tie tack was shaped like a Christmas present, but it also served as a small microphone that Santa could use to talk to Willzer. The last thing Santa did was put a small, inconspicuous receiver in his right ear.

After they'd eaten some more donuts and drank some more coffee, Willzer put on a headset so he could communicate with Santa. Then he got inside a small, cozy, red trunk that was shaped a lot like a school locker.

The trunk had a comfortable chair inside and plenty of breathing room for Willzer. A large, decorative, two-way mirror shaped like a Christmas wreath was built into one side of the trunk. It would provide Willzer a great view of what was going on outside the trunk without anyone being able to see him inside.

Just before they left their suite, Santa put on a Minnesota Vikings parka, snow boots, and some gloves. Then he picked up the trunk using the convenient carrying handle on top.

From inside the trunk, Willzer whispered, "We're on our way."

Santa could hear Willzer loud and clear through the receiver in his ear. "Ho! Ho! Ho! Off we go! This should be an adventure," Santa said excitedly.

After leaving their room, they took the elevator to the ground floor. Ben Dove, a tired, young college student who'd been working at the front desk all night, thought he was imagining things as a big guy who looked like Santa—wearing a Vikings parka—carrying a red trunk—went out the front door of the hotel.

The short walk from the hotel to Jim Coats Elementary School was fabulous. Santa made the coolest crunchy sound as he walked through the snow on the sidewalks. With the bright, newly risen sun reflecting off the snow, the blue sky, and

no wind to speak of, it was a beautiful December morning in North Dakota despite the below zero temperatures.

Occupants in passing cars couldn't help but notice a Santa look-alike walking down the sidewalk with a red trunk in hand. Adding to the peculiarity, they noticed the old guy seemed to be singing to himself or talking to himself.

Actually, Santa and Willzer were having a conversation and testing out their communication devices. "I'm actually finding this quite exhilarating," Santa said. "Risk-taking can be so inspiring ... so much fun!"

"I only hope you feel that way once school starts," answered Willzer, snug as an elf could be inside the cozy trunk.

In a few minutes, Santa was walking past the school playground on the way to the main entrance to Jim Coats Elementary School. As soon as Santa entered the school, a kindergarten teacher passed by on the way to her room. She had her arms full of books, school mail, and student papers—and her coffee cup was balanced precariously on top of the big pile.

Without even thinking, Santa said, "Good morning, Mrs. Volk!"

"Good morning," Mrs. Volk replied, so deep in thought she didn't even notice who'd greeted her. She just kept walking down to her room.

"Santa," Willzer whispered, "don't forget. You're supposed to be a substitute teacher who's never been in this building before. There's no way you could know everyone's names yet. Starting right now, you're Mr. Clausnitzer, substitute teacher."

"Sorry," Santa whispered, "but I still remember bringing Mrs. Volk a Betty Burp Doll when she was just three years old. She was such a nice little girl."

Santa walked into the office carrying the red trunk. He set the trunk down and was immediately greeted by the school's friendly secretary, Mary Stark.

Mary had been the secretary at Jim Coats Elementary for thirty-five years, and she thought she had seen it all during that time. This, however, was definitely a new one for her.

In fact, Mary was a little flustered. "H-h-how can I help you?" she stuttered.

"Hi," said Santa with a big smile. "I'm Mr. Clausnitzer, substituting for Miss Kemper the next couple of days."

Mary blushed. "Did anyone ever tell you that you look a lot like Santa Claus?" she asked.

"Maybe a few times," Santa said with a friendly smile.

Principal Archie Shaw was in his adjoining office with the door open and he could hear this conversation. He got up from his desk to meet his new substitute teacher.

As Archie Shaw walked over to join them, Mary said, "Oh, this is our principal, Mr. Shaw. This is Mr. Clausnitzer. He's going to be Miss Kemper's substitute teacher this week."

"Mr. Clausnitzer, it's so nice of you to do this for us," said Mr. Shaw, shaking Santa's hand. (Actually, Mr. Shaw was thinking—*Oh, no! This guy's not going to make it one hour in Miss Kemper's room. I'm going to be stuck subbing.*)

"Miss Kemper's class can be a real challenge," Mr. Shaw added, trying to smile. "Please let me know if there's anything I can do to help out while you're here at Jim Coats Elementary School." (Actually, he was thinking—*Why didn't I take that job selling playground equipment ten years ago?*)

Abby Lu Kramer, one of Miss Kemper's fourth graders, was buying a lunch ticket in the office and she overheard the fact that this Santa look-alike was going to be her class's substitute. She walked over to where Santa, Mr. Shaw, and Mary Stark were standing, and said, "If it's OK with you, Mr. Shaw, I can show Mr. Clausnitzer where our classroom is before I go outside."

"That's so nice of you, Abby Lu," Mr. Shaw said. "That would be great."

"Thank-you, Abby Lu," said Santa. "I appreciate your kindness."

Santa picked up the red trunk with his right hand, and they left the office. As they walked down the hall toward the three fourth grade classrooms, word spread faster than the speed of light that Miss Kemper's class was getting a substitute teacher who looked just like Santa Claus. Before Abby Lu had even finished guiding Santa to Miss Kemper's classroom, the Hooooshka triplets and almost everyone else on the playground had heard the news.

Seconds later, Brian, Braydon, and Tyler Hooooshka were rounding up all the other fourth graders in Miss Kemper's class. Less than three minutes after that, the Hooooshkas had all of them standing up against the side of the school, as far away from all the rest of the school kids as they could get so no one else could hear what they were saying.

The Hooooshka triplets towered above their smaller classmates, and they glared at them with threatening looks. "Listen!" Tyler hissed. "We want to break our substitute teacher crying record—and you're gonna help us! We wanna get that old geezer to cry before ten o'clock this morning."

"That's right," Braydon Hooooshka growled as he pointed at his classmates, "and all of you are gonna help us—or else!"

"Yeah, you little creeps!" boomed Brian Hooooshka. "Here's what you're all gonna do ..."

Less than five minutes before the outside bell rang, Santa and Willzer found a great place in the back of the room to set the red trunk. From that location, Willzer's view of the whole classroom from inside the trunk was almost perfect.

At 8:30 the outside bell rang, and soon all twenty-three students in Miss Kemper's class came into the room. Santa greeted each of them with a friendly *good morning* as they walked in. He was pleasantly surprised when they politely returned his greeting, then they all sat down quietly in the five rows of desks set up in the classroom.

After Santa led them in the Pledge of Allegiance, everyone sat down quietly again, then looked up at Santa attentively. "Good morning, everyone," said Santa—then he turned around to write **Mr. Clausnitzer** on the board.

Once Santa had his back to the students and had written a few letters, the Hooooshkas immediately triggered the first step of their diabolical plan. Quietly, under the Hooooshkas' threatening stares, every student in class quickly reached into their desks and grabbed an object. Some grabbed a piece of crumpled up paper. Others grabbed something else like a pencil or eraser or roll of Scotch tape. The Hooooshkas reached for the biggest ammunition of all—their big heavy social studies books. Then all the fourth graders cocked their arms back—ready to throw.

From his vantage point, Willzer could see what was going on and he was horrified. Santa could be injured. He had to do something quickly.

"Santa, you're about to get plastered!" Willzer whispered frantically.

Santa turned around—not quite sure what Willzer had just said—at exactly the same time as Braydon Hooooshka whispered loudly, "Fire!"

Phase one of the Hooooshkas' plan was to have everyone throw an object at the marker board close to the substitute teacher—the first time he turned around to write something on the board. It was meant to scare him—but from Willzer's vantage point—it looked much more dangerous than that.

No matter how much the Hoooshkas had threatened their classmates, there's no way most of them were going to throw something even close to their substitute—no matter what the Hoooshkas had said. They either held onto their objects or threw them way off target onto the carpet someplace.

Arly Richau, a tough, wiry kid who was sitting in the back of the middle row, was totally sick of the Hoooshkas. Arly knew he would probably get pounded later, but he didn't care. He threw the roll of Scotch tape he was holding right at the back of the head of the guy sitting in the second seat in the first row—Braydon Hoooshka.

The Hoooshka triplets were right on target with their objects. Their social studies books were well on their way—just about ready to hit close to Santa's face. Without any time to think, Willzer quickly pointed toward the front of the room.

Suddenly, all the objects, from all the fourth graders—including the social studies books that were just about set to bonk close to Santa's head—stopped in midair. The next moment they

all lined up in a neat straight line about two feet off the ground, then floated like some strange parade through the air, finally dropping, one-by-one, into the large waste paper basket next to the teacher's desk.

Most of the students were shocked. The Hooooshka triplets couldn't believe their eyes, and they were determined to give their plan *another* try. This time they grabbed their math books and hurled them right at Santa.

When the Hooooshkas threw their math books, Santa winked. Suddenly the three math books stopped in midair, rose up near the ceiling, then started dancing around like they were doing some strange math book square dance. All the fourth graders looked up and watched in total amazement.

The whole class was utterly astounded—except the Hooooshkas. Brian and Tyler Hooooshka thought they were dreaming. Braydon Hooooshka wasn't sure what was happening, but he decided to do something he'd never done before—run to the office to tell the principal something.

He got out of his desk and ran over to the door, opened it—and he got another stupendous surprise. There was no longer a hall where there should have been one. Instead, all he could see was a blizzard of heavy snow falling—and a horse drawn sleigh dashing directly toward him.

For the first time in a long time, Braydon Hooooshka was scared. He turned right around, closed the classroom door, and just stood there, stunned, with his eyes almost popping out of their sockets.

He looked at his classmates ... he looked at his two confused brothers ... then he looked up at the marker board where Santa had started to write *Mr. Clausnitzer,* but wasn't able to finish. It just said—*Mr. Claus.*

After another few seconds of silence, Braydon finally blurted, "You are Mr. Santa Claus, aren't you!?"

4

There was a stunned silence in the classroom for several seconds after Braydon Hooooshka spoke. It took lots of time for the events of the past few seconds to be absorbed by all those fourth grade minds.

The Hooooshka triplets quickly realized they were in the presence of a power infinitely greater than the three of them. This Santa Claus dude was no one to mess with.

Santa was thinking that his substitute teaching days were most definitely over. My gosh! He hadn't even made it through the first five minutes of his first teaching day! Now, what was he going to do?

Finally, the classroom silence was broken when Tyler Hooooshka asked, "So, Santa. All that stuff I've heard about you isn't a bunch of fairy tales, huh?"

"No, Tyler, it's probably all pretty accurate," Santa replied.

Braydon Hooooshka looked very uncomfortable. "And all that stuff about you knowing if we've been bad or good—that's true, too?" he asked.

"Yup, pretty much," Santa answered.

The Hooooshka triplets were silent, trying to consider all the implications of what they'd just heard.

Finally, Brian Hooooshka asked, "Did you come to Mandan to waste me and my brothers for being so mean all the time?"

"Ho! Ho! Ho!" said Santa. "No, Brian. Miss Kemper had to go to the Mandan Hospital for surgery—but don't worry, she's going to be just fine. She sent me a letter about the situation ... and I thought maybe I could be her substitute teacher for a few days."

Holly Hopkins, a smart girl who wanted to be a teacher since she was in kindergarten—until she met the Hooooshka triplets—spoke up. "You were going to try to be *our* substitute without any previous teaching experience?" she asked.

"Well," Santa explained, "actually, Willzer was going to help me out. I guess the two of us thought we could get through a few days ... but it looks like we barely made it through a few *seconds.*"

"Who's Willzer?" asked Tommy Muscatell, a short, stocky, dark-haired kid who was sitting in the front of the middle row.

"Oh, I'm sorry," Santa said, looking toward the back of the classroom. "Willzer, come on out and meet everyone."

The kids' attention was drawn to the red trunk in the back of the classroom. The fourth graders watched with great anticipation as Willzer slowly opened the door and peeked out with a dubious smile on his face. The eyes of the students got huge and their mouths opened wide as all nine and a half inches of Willzer got out of the trunk and scooted to the front of the room.

Mr.
Claus

"You're one of them elf guys!" Trace Van Pelt exclaimed, unable to control his excitement.

"He's sooooooo cute," Abby Lu whispered.

"Finally, I'm not the shortest kid in the class," Lefty Faris mumbled to himself.

Standing next to Santa in the front of the classroom, Willzer barely reached above Santa's ankles. Many of the fourth graders tried not to giggle—but they couldn't help it.

"Hi, fourth graders," Willzer said.

"Hi, Willzer," they all answered back.

"Oh, thanks for that friendly greeting," Willzer said with a big smile. "I *am* Willzer and I teach at our elementary school at the North Pole. As you probably figured out already, I was going to hide in the red trunk in the back of the classroom where I could communicate with Santa if he needed any help teaching. That's why I'm wearing this headset. Santa's wearing an earpiece, and his little tie tack there is actually a microphone."

Dakota Roush, a tall boy wearing a Dallas Cowboys football jersey, raised his hand. He was the student sitting closest to the waste paper basket.

"Are you the one that made the stuff fly into that garbage can?" he wanted to know.

"Yes," Willzer replied, "I thought someone might hit Santa and hurt him ... and Christmas Eve would be ruined for millions of kids like you all over the world."

"That was cool—and I'm glad you did it," Tyler Hooooshka said. "Uh ... could you two guys still be our substitute teachers till Christmas?"

It was as if Tyler suddenly flipped a switch. For the first time since Halloween, everyone in Miss Kemper's class wanted the same thing, and they instantly put all their fourth grade charm and persuasion in high gear.

"Yeah, would you?" Brian Hooooshka said, looking around at his classmates. "We would all promise to be good, wouldn't we?"

"YES!" everyone replied.

Many in the class were a little freaked out at hearing Brian Hooooshka being the spokesperson for *promising to be good.*

Braydon Hooooshka added, "Hey ... and none of us will tell anyone that we have Santa and an elf substituting in our class."

That remark made everyone in the classroom laugh—including Santa and Willzer.

"See? Who would believe us anyway?" Tommy Muscatell observed.

"Certainly not my parents," Holly Hopkins said.

Lefty Faris mumbled to himself, "My parents still don't believe we ever landed on the moon. How would they ever believe *this?*"

The fourth graders noticed Santa and Willzer seemed to be considering—so they poured it on even more.

"Pleeeeeeeease?"

"It would be the perfect Christmas gift!"

"I'll quit picking on my little brother!"

"I'll even do dishes for the whole year without my mom making me."

"Me and my brothers will give you our BB guns," Brian Hooooshka promised.

"You can have our ropes, too!" Tyler Hooooshka added.

Those BB guns and ropes were the Hooooshka triplets' most prized possessions. They loved shooting at things and tying things up—including each other.

After all the fourth graders had spewed their best persuasive efforts, it was silent as forty-six pleading eyes focused all their attention on Santa and Willzer.

"Willzer, what do you think?" Santa asked.

Willzer shrugged. "I'm willing to give it a try if you are," he said.

"All right," Santa said. "If all of you keep your promises to be good and help Willzer and me out—we'll do it ... and Brian, Tyler, and Braydon—I'll let you keep your BB guns and rope."

All the fourth graders cheered.

Brian Hooooshka raised his hand. "Uh ... Santa ... I have one question," he said softly. "Me and my brothers have been pretty mean—*really* mean—for a long time, and we never believed in you or nothing. Now that we know you're real and everything ... is there any chance you would ever bring us something ... maybe in a couple of years ... if we promise to be really good from now on."

"Ho! Ho! Ho!" Santa said, laughing. "Brian, if you and your brothers start being as good as you can, we might even be able to find a little something up there at the North Pole to bring you *this* Christmas Eve."

The Hooooshka triplets were astonished. They couldn't believe this great deal. Santa was actually going to overlook all the mean stuff they'd ever done if they'd be as good as possible from now on. This was a deal they couldn't pass up. This was the best deal in the whole universe!

"It's a deal!" Brian Hooooshka said. His two brothers nodded their heads energetically and smiled to seal the deal.

At that moment, a great Hooooshka Christmas miracle occurred. The Hooooshka triplets were suddenly filled to the brim and then overflowed with a Christmas spirit like no one had ever seen before.

This was a pretty good deal for all the other fourth graders in Miss Kemper's class, too. They were getting an early Christmas gift that was hard to believe—nice Hooooshkas. Getting Santa and Willzer as substitute teachers till Christmas was unbelievably awesome, too.

Holly Hopkins was as fired up as the rest of them. She immediately raised her hand and asked, "Santa, what are you and Willzer going to teach us this week?"

"Uh ... Willzer and I have some lesson plans," Santa said, "but I'll bet some of you might have other great suggestions for us. Why don't we talk about that right now. I'll write some of your ideas down on the board, and I'll have Willzer lead the discussion."

As the students watched in wonder, Willzer snapped his fingers—and suddenly he was standing on the stool in front of the classroom. Santa picked up a board marker and got ready to write down the students' suggestions.

"Can we make get well cards for Miss Kemper?" Braydon Hooooshka asked.

It was pretty incredible hearing this from a Hooooshka triplet.

"I think that's a great idea," Willzer said as Santa wrote *Miss Kemper Get Well Cards* down on the board. "We can have art class sometime today for that."

Thomas Ladd, who loved math and soccer, asked, "Could you and Santa maybe tell us about the reindeer sometime? Can they really fly, and does Rudolph really have a red nose that glows?"

"I think we can do that, Thomas," Willzer said.

Santa wrote ***The Fantastic Reindeer*** and ***Rudolph's Red Nose*** on the board.

Trace loved to play golf. He asked, "What do you guys do at the North Pole when you're not working? Do you ever play golf?"

"That's a very interesting question, Trace," Willzer said, as Santa wrote it down on the board.

"How do you get all those presents on Santa's sleigh?" Abby Lu asked.

As this discussion was going on, Mr. Shaw walked down the hall, approaching the closed door of Miss Kemper's classroom, expecting to hear total chaos coming from the room by now. He was dreading the fact that he might have to take over the class immediately if things were getting out of control. He crossed his fingers for good luck, put his ear close to the door—could only hear one person speaking— and he quickly walked down the hall, feeling relieved.

No need to peek in. That was good enough for him. He walked back to his office, keeping his fingers crossed the whole time.

After the fourth graders had offered almost a marker board full of good suggestions, Tommy Muscatell said, "It's time for gym class—but we really don't want to go."

"Why not?" Santa asked.

"Well," Tommy explained, "this week, all the other classes get to choose what they want to do 'cause it's Christmas week and everything, but our class doesn't because we've been pretty mean and uncooperative." (Actually, the Hooooshka triplets had been mean and uncooperative.) "We have to do pushups and watch a video on good sportsmanship."

"Is that what you deserve?" Santa wanted to know.

"Yes," the fourth graders answered weakly.

"Not really," Braydon Hooooshka admitted. "Me and my brothers were the only mean ones. We sorta ruined it for everyone else."

"Well," Santa said. "I suggest we go down there and try to be especially good while we're doing the pushups and watching the video. It would be a nice Christmas gift for your teacher, don't you think?"

"OK," the fourth graders responded with very little enthusiasm.

They all lined up and walked down the hall to the gym—Santa leading the way. Willzer stayed back in the classroom for obvious reasons.

When Santa walked into the gym with the class, he introduced himself to Mrs. Feeney, the gym teacher. Mrs. Feeney, who had believed in Santa forever, smiled broadly, thinking to herself how much this handsome gentleman looked like the real Santa—as she imagined he looked, anyway.

All the fourth graders were very quiet as Santa whispered something in Mrs. Feeney's right ear for about thirty seconds. As he was doing this, her smile got bigger and bigger and her face started turning redder and redder.

When Santa finished whispering to her, Mrs. Feeney was obviously more than a little flustered. She quickly tried to regain her composure. She said, "Um … in the spirit of Christmas, I'm going to give you a chance to pick your activity today ... just as long as it isn't dodgeball—but you've got to promise to be good sports."

The Hooooshka triplets had bruised and battered everyone the first and last time the class had played dodgeball. Poor Lefty Faris had been knocked silly by a Brian Hooooshka fastball to his head.

Mrs. Feeney cringed a little as Brian Hooooshka walked up to her. "Mrs. Feeney, we all know me and my brothers were the ones who caused all the trouble for you. We promise we'll be good sports from now on in your class."

"Well ... thank you, Brian," Mrs. Feeney said, not believing what she was hearing. "Uh ... maybe *you'd* like to pick the activity for the day."

"Could you let Lefty pick?" Brian suggested. "I still feel bad about knocking him silly that time."

"Lefty, would you like to pick the activity?" Mrs. Feeney asked.

Lefty Faris perked up. He looked around at his classmates, trying to get some hints from them. "Sure, how about kickball?" he offered.

"Yeah, good idea, Lefty!"

"Yay! Kickball!"

Mrs. Feeney hesitated a little, remembering how many ceiling tiles had been destroyed the last time the Hooooshka triplets played kickball in the gym.

"Uh ... OK," she said. "Maybe San—, I mean, maybe your teacher can be the all-time pitcher— if he wouldn't be too uncomfortable doing that in his suit ..."

When they got back from gym class, Thomas Ladd asked Santa, "What did you whisper in Mrs. Feeney's ear down in the gym?"

Santa smiled. "I merely asked her how her nineteen grandchildren were doing ... and I asked her if she really wanted a University of Nebraska sweatshirt for Christmas. Now, we've got about an hour before you go to lunch. What should we do next?"

"Could Willzer and you do a little more magic for us?" Dakota Roush asked.

"Well, I guess so," Santa said.

Santa and Willzer talked things over for about thirty seconds.

"OK," said Santa, "here's something you might like. Willzer and I need all of you to make sure you're sitting up straight in your desks and holding on tightly."

Santa smiled and winked his right eye. Willzer waved his right hand over the entire room. All of a sudden, the desks rose into the air about one foot off the ground. Then, they all started flying all over the room, never running into each other. It was like flying bumper cars without all the collisions.

The fourth graders were all having the best time *ever.* What a blast!

Unfortunately, Archie Shaw chose that moment to walk by Miss Kemper's room. He heard lots of commotion this time and feared the Hooooshkas had tied up the substitute teacher or something. He'd have to peek in—it was his job.

He turned the doorknob slowly, intending to open the door just a crack. Willzer spotted the movement out of the corner of his eye and

pointed toward the door, making it impossible for Mr. Shaw to open it.

Willzer got Santa's attention, and whispered, "The principal's at the door."

In a few seconds, Willzer and Santa magically returned all the desks to their normal positions and put their index fingers to their mouths—a signal for all the fourth graders to be quiet. Then Willzer snapped his fingers and disappeared.

Mr. Shaw thought the door was stuck so he gave it one big final push, using all the strength he could muster. He burst in, almost falling on the floor as he stumbled into the classroom.

When Mr. Shaw regained his balance, he looked around the room. Mr. Clausnitzer was teaching a lesson on fractions. All the students seemed to be following the lesson attentively.

"Uh … things seem to be going well here," Mr. Shaw finally managed to say. "I'm sorry for the interruption … uh … keep up the good work."

The principal left the room, totally baffled and very suspicious.

5

After school was out and all the students had left, Willzer got into the red trunk. Santa picked it up and started walking back to the Lewis and Clark Hotel.

As they were walking along, Santa said, "I must tell you, Willzer, I'm totally exhausted ... but I think it's been one of the most exciting days of my life." Santa yawned. "I've always had a lot of respect for what you teachers do, but I never knew how tough the job really was."

"Well, you did a great job today, Santa," said Willzer. "We had a strange start, but we made some adjustments and things worked out quite well—if I do say so myself."

"Thanks for saving me at the beginning of the day," Santa said.

"You're so welcome, Santa," Willzer replied. "I've learned to expect the unexpected since I started teaching, but even I was surprised at what happened."

As soon as they got back to their room at the hotel, Willzer said, "Santa, you'd better call Mrs. Claus right now. I'll bet she's been worrying about us all day."

"I'll do that," said Santa. "I've got to talk to Ziggy and Patrick, too." Santa reached into a nearby drawer and pulled out his candy cane phone. He pressed one button.

"Hello, Dear! It's your loving, cuddly teacher husband." Santa chuckled.

"Hi, Honey. I've been worrying about you all day. How did your first day of teaching go?"

"Well ... Willzer and I got off to a rather dubious start, but by the end of the day, all the fourth graders seemed to be getting along, and we were having a great time!"

"What did you do all day?"

"You won't believe all the things we accomplished. Let's see ... in the morning, we all got acquainted and the fourth graders gave Willzer and me some suggestions regarding things they'd like to be taught during this short Christmas week. Later, I even played all-time pitcher during gym class. In the afternoon we had art class where the students made some marvelous get well cards for Miss Kemper. Willzer and I also taught math and science lessons that were quite invigorating."

"I'll bet Willzer was extremely helpful."

"More than you can ever imagine, Dear."

"Did any of the students try to test you like they usually do when there's a substitute teacher?"

"At first, yes. But once we got through all of that, things went much better ... super, in fact!"

"So ... do you have anything special planned for tomorrow?"

"Yes, we do. In fact, I need to talk to Ziggy and Patrick about that after I'm done talking to you. How are things going at the North Pole?"

"Everything's going well here. Everyone's working hard on last minute stuff. What are Willzer and you doing tonight?"

"I think we're going to get a pizza delivered from this place called A&B Pizza. A few of Mandan's children have left me cold pieces of A&B pizza on Christmas Eve in the past, and I thought it was tremendous. I'd like to try a hot pizza for a change. After that, we'll probably just relax and enjoy the wonderful view from our fourth story window. Honey, it looks like much of the Christmas activity in Mandan takes place right across the street from our hotel."

"What's going on?"

"Well, there's a great old train depot surrounded by an enormous park with a gigantic ice skating rink and huge trees everywhere. It's not dark yet, but everything seems to be decorated with thousands of lights. There's even a small stage set up—probably for singing groups and things. I'll bet it's all going to be beautiful when it gets dark."

"Sounds like so much fun. I wish I was there to share it with you."

"So do I. We'll be sure to take some great pictures to show you when we return."

"That would be splendid ... Well, you'd better call Ziggy and Patrick now ... but please keep in touch, and please save some of your energy for Christmas Eve."

"I will, Dear ... I love you."

"I love you, too. Bye."

"Bye."

Santa pressed another button on his candy cane phone.

"Hi, Ziggy. This is Santa."

"Hi, Santa. How did things go today?"

"We had a little problem early on, but things moved along nicely after that. Uh ... Ziggy. Willzer and I wondered if you could spare three elves for the next two days. We'd need some of the best toy makers who like to work with kids."

"That might be possible. What do you have in mind?"

"Well, Willzer and I thought we'd do a special toy making project with the fourth graders tomorrow."

"Very well. Just let me know what I need to do."

"All right. I'll talk to Patrick next and get right back to you."

"Sounds good. I'll talk to you later, Santa."

"Thanks, Ziggy. Good-bye."

"Bye, Santa."

Santa pressed another button on his phone.

"Patrick, this is Santa. How are things going with your snowmaking machine?"

"*Frosty,* Santa. I mean, the other scientists and I decided to name our machine Frosty. I-I've got some good news and some bad news about Frosty."

"Why don't you give me the good news first."

"Well, the good news is ... we attached Frosty to the back of the sleigh successfully and tested him while flying near the North Pole. He worked like a dream for almost two hours—except for the little hiccup. That's the bad news."

"What hiccup?"

"Well, we'd been testing for almost two hours. Frosty was producing fantastic snowflakes—then suddenly he made a funny sound—something like a hiccup. After that, something sorta strange happened."

"What was that?"

"Well, after the hiccup, Frosty started making *purple* snowflakes …We don't really want anyone to have a purple Christmas, do we, Santa? It just wouldn't be right."

Santa giggled. "Purple wouldn't be good," he said. "Not a lot of children are dreaming of a purple Christmas."

"That's for sure, Santa. Anyway, the other scientists and I are going to work all night to try to fix the perplexing purple problem. Tomorrow we plan to test Frosty further south of here in a warmer climate to see how he works in those conditions."

"Patrick, how would you like to stop by here on the way tomorrow morning with three of my elves?"

"What are you planning on doing, Santa?"

"We've got a toy making project in mind for school tomorrow, but Willzer and I need more help."

"Oh, sounds interesting. I'll let Ethan know about it, too."

"I'll call you later after I talk to Ziggy. Keep up the good work, Patrick."

"Thanks, Santa. Bye."

Around the dinner tables in certain Mandan houses occupied by Miss Kemper's fourth graders and their families, there were some interesting conversations taking place. Trace Van Pelt was enjoying a steak dinner at home, along with his parents and his third grade brother, Bo.

"How did the day go in school, boys?" Mr. Van Pelt asked.

"Fine," Bo said, "but Trace had a substitute that looks just like Santa Claus!"

"Is that right, Trace?" Mrs. Van Pelt asked.

"Yes, Mom," Trace replied, wanting to tell his parents that the substitute not only *looked* just like Santa but he *was* Santa—but he knew better. "Miss Kemper is having some kind of surgery, so Mr. Clausnitzer is our substitute for a few days," said Trace.

"Mr. Clausnitzer, huh? How's he doing?" Trace's dad wanted to know. "Can he control the Hoooshka triplets at all?"

"Yes, he's doing a really good job," Trace replied.

"Do you know where this Mr. Clausnitzer comes from?" Trace's mom asked. She knew some Clausnitzers from nearby Bismarck and wondered if they might be related to the substitute.

Trace hesitated before speaking, not wanting to lie to his parents but not wishing to give them too much information either. "He lives somewhere north of Mandan," Trace finally said. "I think Miss Kemper knows him … and she asked him to substitute for her until Christmas."

"Oh, that's nice …"

Abby Lu's dad was a reporter for *The Mandan News*, and Abby Lu knew she had a once in a lifetime story for her dad—but there was no way she was going to give it to him. Two more days with Santa and Willzer were much more important than her dad's newspaper.

Besides, what would happen if her dad wrote a front page story about Santa and a little elf named Willzer substitute teaching in Mandan? It would be a nightmare. Abby Lu could just picture reporters chasing Santa and Willzer all around town.

"Abby Lu, how did everything go in school today?" her dad asked.

"Good. We had a substitute, Mr. Clausnitzer, and he did a really good job—how about those Minnesota Vikings, Dad ..."

At the Hooooshka house, Brian, Braydon, and Tyler had just cut down a four foot pine tree from a nearby field, and they were carrying it into their house. When they got it inside, they placed it upright in a Christmas tree stand made out of an old coffee can filled with dirt.

After that, the boys ran around the house looking for stuff to make Christmas tree decorations. Among other things, they found some aluminum foil, a couple of old fishing lures, and some pieces of green construction paper.

Brian turned on the old clock radio in the kitchen, and he found a station playing some Christmas music. For the next two hours, the Hooooshka triplets sat around the card table in their small living room and made crude decorations for their small Christmas tree.

Guess what? The Hooooshka triplets didn't fight once the whole time. It was another Hooooshka Christmas miracle.

6

Santa's sleigh took off from the North Pole in the wee hours of the morning on December 22nd. At the time of departure, Dewey reported a crisp, clear twenty-five below zero at the North Pole, and he forecast perfect flying weather all the way to Mandan.

The sleigh was rather full that morning. Ethan and Patrick were joined by Kristin, Olivia, and Drake— the three elves who'd volunteered to help Santa and Willzer.

This was a really big deal for those three. It was the first time any of them had ventured so far from the North Pole.

"Let's fly to Mandan more or less the same way we took yesterday," Ethan called out to the reindeer.

All the reindeer definitely approved of the flight plan.

"Good call, Ethan," Cupid bellowed.

"Yeah, way to go, Ethan!" Blitzen added.

After they'd flown as far as Edmonton, Santa contacted the sleigh from the hotel room in Mandan. "This is Santa—calling the sleigh. Come in, please."

"Good morning, Santa," Ethan replied. "We're currently flying over that huge shopping center in Edmonton with all the waterslides you like so much. We'll be landing in Mandan in just a few minutes. Save us some donuts, please."

"We will," said Santa. "Do you have everything we need on board?"

"Yes, we double-checked everything," Ethan answered. "We've got all the toy-making supplies you'll need ... and Kristin, Olivia, and Drake are right here, anxious to work with the fourth graders there in Mandan."

"Fabulous!" said Santa. "Have Patrick and you decided where you're going to test Frosty today after you stop here in Mandan?"

"A bunch of us scientists were discussing that late last night, Santa," said Patrick. "We wanted to find an isolated area someplace—where it's at least sixty degrees warmer than yesterday's test conditions. We think we've found a perfect place northeast of El Paso, Texas. They have fifty degree temps forecast for the day, and our satellite photos indicate almost no one's living in that area. There are just one or two shacks in hundreds of square miles."

"Sounds like you've found an excellent place," Santa said. "I hope your tests go perfectly today."

"Me too, Santa," said Patrick. "By the way, Santa, I think we fixed the purple snowflakes hiccup. We were up most of the night, but it will be worth it if the problem's fixed."

"That's for sure," agreed Santa. "Think of all the happy children who might be seeing their first *white* snow at Christmas time this year."

"You're right, Santa," said Patrick. "That would be awesome."

Less than twenty minutes later, Willzer and Santa were waiting as Santa's sleigh landed on top of the Lewis and Clark Hotel. Immediately, everyone got to work unloading the sleigh.

As soon as they were done, Ethan said, "Patrick and I better grab a couple donuts and take off right away so we can make the trip down to Texas in the dark. We want to attract as little attention as possible."

"Good idea," said Santa.

Ethan and Patrick got back on board the sleigh. Everyone waved as they took off from the rooftop.

Two blocks away, Mayor Bob Dykshoorn was walking down Main Street as usual, and he had the same whooshing sensation above his head as he'd experienced the morning before.

Quickly, he looked up and saw a small red light at the front of whatever whizzed above him—then he thought he heard an animal sneezing. The next moment, a small trail of light zipped into the sky and disappeared.

The mayor just shook his head. *Yes, a vacation to Hawaii may be in order after Christmas,* he thought.

When it was time to go to school, Santa called the front desk and asked if someone would please call a taxi and send a bellboy up to the room. Ben Dove got up to the room a few minutes later, and his eyes got huge when he saw the two large red trunks lying near the door.

"Looks like you have a big project planned for those kids today," Ben observed.

"Yes, Ben," Santa replied with a big smile, still remembering the Suzie Homemaker oven he'd brought Ben so many Christmases ago.

Santa helped Ben load the two heavy red trunks on his cart. From there, they took the elevator downstairs and went outside where a taxi was already waiting out front.

Taxi driver Wally Joersz got out of his car and opened up the trunk of his taxi. "To the airport?" Wally asked Santa as he looked at the two large red trunks. "I think we'll have to put one of those in the backseat," he noted.

"No, to Jim Coats Elementary School," Santa replied. "And ... could you put that larger one there in the backseat."

"Sure," Wally said.

Wally, Ben, and Santa all had to pitch in to get the two heavy trunks in the car. The trunk with the four elves inside was put in the backseat.

Wally said, "You must have a real doozy of a project planned for the kids today."

"Yup," said Santa, "a huge craft project."

"I wish I could be in your class today," said Wally. "I always liked art class—and recess."

Meanwhile, in the desert near El Paso, Ethan and Patrick were beginning their second day testing Frosty. On the flight down to Texas, Ethan had flown the sleigh right through the Gateway Arch in St. Louis. It was something Santa probably would have frowned upon, but it had been quite a thrill for Patrick and Ethan—*and* the reindeer.

Santa attracted lots of attention as he entered the school with the two big red trunks. Wally helped Santa roll them down to Miss Kemper's room, and Santa rewarded him with a nice tip when they were done.

When the morning bell rang outside, Miss Kemper's students quickly ran from the playground and lined up near the entrance. They could hardly wait to get into the school, sensing they were about to have one of the most exciting days of their lives.

Miss Kemper's fourth graders walked anxiously down the hall to the classroom, took their coats and boots off as quickly as possible at the coat rack in the hall, then walked into the room. Santa was waiting by the door to greet each of them as they walked in.

"Good morning, *Mr. Clausnitzer,*" Tyler Hooooshka said with a huge smile. It looked like Tyler had even washed his face that morning— something he rarely did.

"Good morning, Tyler," Santa replied.

"Good morning, Mr. Clausnitzer," Braydon Hooooshka said as he walked by Santa.

"Good morning, Braydon," said Santa.

Brian Hooooshka walked by next and handed Santa a little box wrapped rather creatively in aluminum foil and masking tape. "Me and my brothers made a little something for the classroom Christmas tree last night," Brian said proudly. "You can put it on the tree sometime if you like."

"Why, thank-you," Santa said with a big smile. "I'll do that sometime early this morning."

Soon, all of Miss Kemper's fourth graders had gone to their desks and were trying to settle down, but it was absolutely impossible. For all of them, this was a million times better than the Halloween party. This was even a thousand times better than the last day of school. It was even a hundred times better than opening up gifts on Christmas Eve.

After they said the Pledge of Allegiance, Santa opened up the gift the Hooooshkas had given him earlier, as all the fourth graders watched with anticipation.

"Who gave you that?" Arly Richau asked.

"Brian, Braydon, and Tyler made it for our classroom Christmas tree," Santa answered, as he held up the homemade ornament, an unusual combination of fishing lure, aluminum foil, and green construction paper. "It's such a wonderful gift, and it's a perfect introduction to what we're going to be doing today."

"Wow! That's cool. Are we going to make Christmas tree ornaments?" Dakota Roush inquired.

"Actually, all of you are going to get a chance to find out exactly what it's like to be an elf at the North Pole—making all those gifts and everything. Only, instead of working at the North Pole, Willzer and I brought the North Pole to you."

"Where *is* Willzer?" Holly Hopkins asked.

"Oh ... Willzer's here," Santa said, glancing toward the back of the room. "He's going to help us—along with three of his friends."

The students all looked toward the back of the room where the two big red trunks were sitting. As the fourth graders watched in suspense, the door of the larger trunk opened, and four elves emerged and walked to the front of the room. The kids oohed and aahed with excitement and surprise.

"As you can see," said Santa, "Willzer and I have a few more friends who will be helping us this morning."

The four elves stood next to Santa in the front of the classroom. First, there was Willzer—nine and a half inches tall. Next to Willzer was Kristin—just under four feet in height. Next to Kristin were Olivia and Drake, both slightly under three feet tall.

Santa introduced his friends. "Of course, you've already met Willzer," he began. "Next to Willzer is Kristin. She's leader of the Letters to Santa Team at the North Pole and she, like the others, volunteered to come here to help today."

Kristin waved and smiled. "Hi," she said.

"Next to Kristin is Olivia," Santa continued. "She's actually a sixth grader at North Pole Middle School, and she's one of the most gifted artists there." Olivia waved and smiled, then gave thumbs up.

"Hi, everyone," she said in her sweet voice.

"Finally, next to Olivia is Drake," said Santa. "Drake's already one of the best toy makers at the North Pole and he's just a first grader this year."

Drake smiled—then he did a perfect back flip to the delight of everyone. The whole class cheered enthusiastically.

Lefty Faris raised his hand, "Santa, I'm feeling taller every day," he said.

Everyone laughed.

Willzer explained, "Today, Santa, Kristin, Olivia, Drake, and I are going to help you make all sorts of special gifts for some extra special people for Christmas."

Abby Lu looked worried. "I'm really lousy at making things and putting things together, Willzer," she said.

"Abby Lu, you have nothing to worry about," said Willzer. "You're all going to have almost the same magical toy-making skills as our best elves do."

"Are you going to zap us with a magical spell or something?" Brian Hooooshka asked.

"Ho! Ho! Ho!" Santa laughed. "There will be no zapping in this classroom, Brian. But we are going to give you a little magical help."

"How?" Tommy Muscatell asked.

"Just like *this*," Santa said as he gave Tommy a little wink.

"I didn't feel anything," said Tommy.

Santa walked over to an old overhead projector in the corner of the room. "Tommy, I want you to come over here and take this thing apart, then put it back together again."

Tommy hesitated, but he soon got out of his desk and walked over to the overhead projector. As soon as he touched the machine, there was a fast-motioned flurry of activity as Tommy Muscatell totally disassembled and then reassembled the overhead projector in less than thirty seconds as the fourth graders watched in amazement. Then Tommy turned it on and it actually worked.

When Tommy was finished, Trace Van Pelt said, "That was beyond cool—but where are we going to get all the supplies and stuff to make a bunch of toys?"

Santa walked to the back of the classroom and opened up the door of the smaller red trunk. He took out the loaded big red cloth bag inside and walked up to the front of the classroom, carrying it over his shoulder.

"Everything we need is right in here," Santa said.

"In that one bag?" Abby Lu asked.

"In that one bag," Santa replied.

"Is that your *official* red bag?" Arly Richau wanted to know.

"That's right, Arly," Santa answered. "Why don't you come up and help me unload it. You might be surprised at what's inside."

Arly walked up to the front of the classroom and started pulling things out of the red bag. He handed the stuff to the elves, who took the supplies and placed them on students' desks, on the floor, and everywhere else they could find room.

"That bag's like a black hole! There's no bottom to it!" Thomas Ladd exclaimed. "Santa, now I see how you get millions of gifts on your sleigh at one time."

"That's right, Thomas," Santa said.

After the room was full of supplies, the elves

divided the room into toy-making groups. Each elf took a group of five or six students.

Santa walked closer to the classroom door carrying his red bag, now empty. "While you're working on your toys," Santa explained, "I'm going to be over here by the door, just in case we have any unexpected visitors. There are two other things I'll be doing over here. First, I'm going to call you over one at a time and have you give a little Christmas message to Miss Kemper into the tape recorder. Second, when you finish making a toy, I want you to bring it over to me and put it in my red bag. Is everyone ready to begin?"

"YES!"

Santa waved his hand over the classroom. "1 … 2 … 3 … **GO!**"

Immediately, the fourth graders started making hundreds of toys and other gifts like they had been doing it forever—in fast motion. When they were done making a gift, they took it over and put it into Santa's red bag—also in fast motion.

Meanwhile, Archie Shaw was sitting in his office. He hadn't slept at all last night. He'd had weird dreams about Santa substitute teaching in *his* school. Could that possibly be true?

Finally, he couldn't stand it any longer. He had to find out. He had to see what was going on in Miss Kemper's room. Maybe he should just take Mr. Clausnitzer aside and ask him right out who he really was.

Mr. Shaw walked down the hall toward the fourth grade classrooms, his hand sweating from extreme nervousness. As he slowly approached the door of Miss Kemper's room, he still wasn't sure whether he wanted to go inside or turn around and go back to his office. He got his nerve up, then slowly turned the doorknob.

Santa saw the doorknob turn, and he knew exactly who was about to enter the room. He let Mr. Shaw come right in, greeting him at the door. "Mr. Shaw, come on in and take a look at what the boys and girls are working on," Santa said.

Mr. Shaw entered the room, froze, looked around, and tried to absorb all of the fast motioned toy-making going on in the room. His jaw dropped and his eyes got as big as chocolate drop cookies. He was totally perplexed, dumbfounded, surprised, and even a little afraid.

Just when Mr. Shaw was about to faint, Santa put a comforting arm on the principal's shoulder to steady him. Then Santa whispered into Mr. Shaw's ear, "Do you think you could arrange for us to get a school bus for tomorrow morning? I'd like to take the boys and girls on a little field trip if I may."

"Uh ... sure, Santa," Mr. Shaw answered weakly. "When would you need that th-tha-that bus?"

That night at the Lewis and Clark Hotel, Santa called Mrs. Claus.

"How did your day go and what are you doing tonight?" Mrs. Claus asked.

"The day in school was great! Right now, the elves and I are watching *Miracle on 34th Street* and eating some delicious burgers and fries we had delivered from a place called Ohm's Hamburgers a few blocks away. Mandan Drug right across the street delivered some delicious shakes. Would you believe they have a real soda fountain there? Anyway, we're also enjoying all the Christmas activities in the park across the street. Honey, there's a large group of children singing beautiful Christmas carols on the stage out there right now. There are dozens of people ice skating—the lights are all sparkling—it's so beautiful!"

"What do you have planned for tomorrow, Dear?"

"Tomorrow's the last day of school before vacation, so students get out at noon. We've got a field trip planned in the morning that the boys and girls will never forget. After that, the elves and I will be flying back to the North Pole ..."

Santa called Patrick after that.

"Hi, Patrick. How did things go today?"

"We're back at the North Pole ... and I've got some good news and some bad news again, Santa."

"Let's start with the good news."

"OK. The good news is ... no more purple snowflakes ... but the bad news is ... another little hiccup occurred. This time, Frosty made little snowmen that fell to the earth. Quite cute, but we

need to get it fixed. If we dropped little snowmen onto some town on Christmas Eve, we could do some serious damage—and we've only got one more day to fix it, Santa! We're running out of time!"

"Try to calm down, Patrick. I've got all the confidence in the world in you and your scientists. Just do the best you can."

"We will, Santa ..."

7

It was two o'clock in the morning on December 23rd—the last day of school before Christmas vacation—the day before Christmas Eve.

At the North Pole, Ethan and Patrick took off in Santa's sleigh. Their destination—Lake Okeechobee in Florida. This would be their last chance to test Frosty before Christmas Eve.

At the Lewis and Clark Hotel, Santa and his four elves were sleeping soundly, but it was a different situation in principal Archie Shaw's house on Division Street in Mandan. Mr. Shaw was lying wide awake in bed, trying to comprehend all the implications of what was going on at his school. Santa was a substitute teacher there, for goodness sakes—and there were a bunch of elves acting as teaching assistants. He'd definitely not been trained for this type of situation.

All of Miss Kemper's fourth graders were exhausted from all the toy-making they'd done in school the previous day. They were sleeping like logs.

Santa arrived in Wally Joersz's taxi at Jim Coats Elementary School that morning with the red trunk that had the four elves inside. Mr. Shaw was waiting anxiously by the front entrance to the school. He ran over to the taxi as Wally was sliding the trunk out of the backseat.

"Good morning, Mr. Clausnitzer," Mr. Shaw said nervously. "I got the bus you wanted. It's over there right now." He pointed to a bus parked nearby with its engine running. "I was just wondering … could I please come along with you wherever you're going?"

Shortly after school started, Santa and Mr. Shaw led Miss Kemper's class out the front doors of the school. As they walked toward the school bus, Santa was carrying his red bag over his shoulder, and Mr. Shaw was rolling the large red trunk to the bus on its handy wheels.

Tiny, a longtime bus driver of giant proportions who knew practically every student in Mandan by name, was waiting by the bus's door. He took the red trunk from Mr. Shaw and lifted it into the bus effortlessly, like it was just a big piece of styrofoam.

In what had to be the deepest voice on the planet, Tiny greeted everyone as they boarded the bus. **"Hi, Arly,"** he said with a friendly smile on his face. **"How's the wrestling going?"**

"Hi, Tiny," Arly said with a big smile. "It's going great."

"Good morning, Holly," Tiny said. **"How are you doing?"**

"Great, Tiny," Holly replied as she boarded the bus.

Santa was the last to get on board. "I'm Mr. Clausnitzer," Santa said, reaching out to shake hands with Tiny. Santa's hand was actually only half the size of Tiny's.

Tiny winked his right eye. "Sure, you are," he whispered. "Where are we headed this fine morning, *Mr. Clausnitzer?*"

"To the Mandan Hospital," Santa replied, still standing in front of the bus, holding his red bag.

"Great!" Tiny boomed. **"We'll be there in ten minutes."**

Braydon Hooooshka was sitting with Tommy Muscatell in the second row of seats in the front of the bus and he overheard Santa mention the Mandan Hospital. "Are we going to see Miss Kemper?" Braydon asked excitedly.

"That's right," Santa said, finally putting his red bag down in front of the bus. "We're going to visit some other special people there, too. You'll have a chance to give them some of the gifts you made yesterday."

"Do you mean the kids in the hospital?" Tommy Muscatell guessed. "Do we get to give *them* the gifts we made?"

"You're way too smart for me," Santa said. "That's *exactly* what we're going to do."

There was lots of cheering on the bus as everyone got the word.

As soon as Santa sat down, Tiny got the bus underway. They hadn't driven one block when Holly Hopkins started singing:

Oh! You better watch out,
You better not cry,
You better not pout,
I'm telling you why:
Santa Claus is coming to town!

The other students soon joined in with Holly, and they all sang the song with great joy. When they got to the *Santa Claus* part of the song, all the fourth graders pointed toward Santa.

Tiny eventually joined in the singing. His deep, booming voice rattled the windows of the school bus.

After singing the song five times, Brian Hooooshka started singing *Rudolph the Red*

Nosed Reindeer. When they got to the word *Santa*—all the students pointed at Santa Claus in the front of the bus again.

By the time they'd sung the Rudolph song five times, they arrived at the Mandan Hospital. Tiny drove the bus as close to the front door as he could.

After that, Tiny unloaded the red trunk, and Mr. Shaw rolled it into the hospital, then down to the cafeteria. Meanwhile, Santa and the fourth graders all walked into the hospital, then right over to the receptionist's area. Santa was carrying his big stuffed red bag over his shoulder.

When Mr. Shaw rolled the trunk into the cafeteria, he noticed one doctor sitting in a chair at a small table. It was seventy-year-old Dr. Blumenthal, who was sleeping soundly, his head bobbing about as he inhaled and exhaled.

Mr. Shaw set the trunk down, opened the door, and the elves got out. Immediately they began working their magic, transforming the room from its drab surroundings to a true Christmas wonderland.

While the elves continued working, Mr. Shaw walked out of the cafeteria and rushed to join the rest of the group. By the time Mr. Shaw caught up with them, Santa and the fourth graders were walking up the steps to the second floor of the hospital. Tiny, who had parked the bus, also joined them at the top of the steps.

They all headed for Room 225. Tiny and the fourth graders waited in a lounge across the hall from the room while Santa and Mr. Shaw were led into Miss Kemper's room by nurse Carla Allbrite.

"You have two extremely handsome visitors," Carla said to Miss Kemper with a big smile.

When Miss Kemper looked up from the pages of the book she was reading and spotted Santa and Mr. Shaw's smiling faces, she said, "Oh, my! It's so good to see you! ...Where are my fourth graders?"

"They're right across the hall waiting for you in the lounge," Mr. Shaw said. "Can you come over and see them for a few minutes?"

"She sure can," nurse Carla answered quickly. "I'll go get a wheelchair."

"How have things been going in school?" Miss Kemper wanted to know.

Santa smiled. "They're going fine, but there's no way I could handle another day," he said. "It's an exhausting job—and I had four elves helping me. I don't know how you can do it, Miss Kemper. How are you feeling?"

"So much better now that you're all here," she replied. "My operation went really well, but Dr. Wheeler says I still have to stay in the hospital a few more days."

Soon, Carla came into the room with the wheelchair. She wheeled Miss Kemper across the hall, as Mr. Shaw and Santa walked behind them.

As soon as the fourth graders saw Miss Kemper enter the room, they all cheered enthusiastically. Brian Hooooshka walked over to Miss Kemper, holding something in his hands behind his back. "Miss Kemper, me and my brothers are sorry for being brats all the time. Santa and his elves have shown us what dorks we've been. We promise we'll be nothing but lots of help to you from now on; we'll help make this year the best year you ever had. Oh—and all of us in your class helped make you this gift."

Brian handed a neatly wrapped gift to Miss Kemper as everyone cheered.

"Oh, wow!" Miss Kemper said, her eyes beginning to tear up. "This is so wonderful!"

Miss Kemper opened the gift slowly as everyone watched with great anticipation. When she saw the beautiful music box inside, tears flowed from her eyes.

"It's so beautiful," she said. "There's even a small snow globe on top."

"Please open it," Abby Lu pleaded.

Miss Kemper slowly opened the music box, and she got a huge surprise. The music box started playing her favorite Christmas song, *Silent Night*—then special Christmas messages from each of her students could be heard as the music continued playing softly in the background.

"Miss Kemper, you're the best! You explain things really well and make them simple for me. Merry Christmas from Dakota Roush."

"Hi, Miss Kemper. This is Thomas Ladd. I like you because you're always nice, even when you must be having a bad day—and you wear the prettiest clothes."

"Merry Christmas, Miss Kemper. I hope I can be half as good a teacher as you some day. I love you. Oh, this is Holly."

"Hi, Miss Kemper! It's Lefty. I hope you're feeling better. You make learning fun. I used to hate reading, but now it's my best subject other than math. Have a great Christmas!"

"Hi, Miss Kemper. It's Arly. You're the first teacher to ever go to my wrestling matches and I really like that. You're awesome!"

"Have a Merry Christmas, Miss Kemper. This is Brian Hooooshka. I promise me and my brothers will be good the rest of the year. We're sorry for being such creeps before. Uh—Merry Christmas again and a Happy New Year, too."

Students waited eagerly for their message to be played. Santa kept handing Kleenex to Miss Kemper and Tiny, who were crying the whole time.

After all the messages had been played, Santa looked at Carla and asked, "I wonder if Miss Kemper and you could join us down in the cafeteria for a little party now?"

"I never pass up a party," Carla said.

"I'd love to," said Miss Kemper.

Carla pushed Miss Kemper toward the elevator in the wheelchair, and everyone else took the stairs. They all joined up at the cafeteria door.

"You're all going to love this!" Mr. Shaw said as he held the door open for everyone.

What they saw inside when they walked in was truly wondrous! The elves had transformed the cafeteria into a Christmas wonderland of toys, music, lights, and color. All the kids who were in the hospital were already enjoying the party of a lifetime!

Just then, Dr. Blumenthal finally woke up from his deep sleep. He looked around ... tried to make sense of what was going on ... then he started to fall out of his chair. Tiny ran over and caught him just in time!

After that, Miss Kemper's students and Tiny helped Santa and his elves pull gifts out of Santa's bag and hand them out to the children. Miss Kemper watched everything going on with a look of pure joy in her eyes.

Tyler Hooooshka handed out a large box wrapped in pretty blue paper to a twelve-year-old named Mike Kern, who'd broken an arm and a leg while skiing at Huff Hills south of Mandan.

Mike was thrilled when he opened the present and saw the remote control airplane he'd wanted for Christmas. "It's just what I wanted!" he cried.

Tyler smiled, looking very proud. "I'm so glad you like it," he said. "I actually got to help make it for you yesterday."

Abby Lu handed a box wrapped in red paper to Nancy Greeno, a first grader who was recovering from a bad case of the flu. "I love these!" Nancy exclaimed when she'd unwrapped a pair of new hockey skates. "They're perfect!" Nancy gave Abby Lu a big hug.

Abby explained, "I put a little extra padding in both skates. You should get fewer blisters than you did with your last pair."

"How did you know about that?" Nancy wanted to know.

"Oh, a little elf told me," Abby Lu replied with a big smile.

After the party was over and everyone said good-bye to Miss Kemper, they all drove back to school in the bus. Once they got to their classroom, there was just enough time for some quick good-byes before the noon dismissal.

"Santa, this has been the best time of my life," Abby Lu said.

"Yeah, I don't want you to leave," Tommy added, trying to hold back the tears.

Even tough guy Arly Richau was crying. "I didn't want this time with the elves and you to ever end," he said.

"There's no need for any of you to cry," said Santa. "You know the elves and I will be keeping track of all of you *forever.*"

Tyler Hooooshka said, "Santa, me and my brothers will be staying up all night tomorrow just in case you come to our house."

"Oh, I'll be dropping by, Tyler," Santa said.

"I'm staying up, too," Thomas Ladd said.

"Me, too," added Tommy Muscatell.

"Me, too," Abby Lu insisted.

"Me, too. And I plan on leaving you some great cookies and milk," said Lefty.

Mr. Shaw came in the classroom and gave Santa a big hug. Santa said, "Archie, thanks for everything. I'll be dropping by your place on Division Street tomorrow night. If you can arrange it, how about some chocolate chip cookies this year? No rice cakes, please."

After the school had emptied, Wally Joersz was waiting for Santa in his taxi in front of the school.

"Where to?" Wally asked Santa after they'd loaded up and were on their way.

"Back to the hotel to pick up the rest of our luggage—then out to Fort Lincoln near the blockhouses," Santa replied.

Wally looked confused. "Huh? There's nothing out there this time of the year but snow," he said.

"That's perfect," said Santa. "We thought it would be a great place to catch our flight back home … it won't attract any attention. We're getting picked up and returning to the North Pole this afternoon. We're kind of busy tomorrow, you know."

Wally looked totally befuddled.

"Wally, you're going to figure it out pretty soon anyway, so I might as well tell you now. I'm Santa Claus, and my sleigh and reindeer are on their way here to pick us up."

"Who's *us?*" Wally wanted to know.

"*Us* is the four elves who are in the red trunk in the backseat of your car right now—and me," Santa explained.

The taxi swerved as Wally turned his head to get a good look at the red trunk in his backseat.

"There are four elves in that trunk back there?" Wally asked.

"That's right, Wally," Santa replied. "Maybe you should pull over to the curb here, and I'll let you meet them."

"Yeah, Wally," came Olivia's voice from inside the trunk. "We don't want you to get in an accident." All the elves giggled.

Wally managed to park his car. Suddenly, the red trunk popped open and all the elves cried, "Hi Wally!"

Wally looked like he was about to faint. He looked over at Santa, then said weakly, "So, you really are Santa."

"Yes, Wally."

"And your sleigh and reindeer are on their way to Fort Lincoln right now?"

"Yes, at this very minute they're probably over the Linton, North Dakota, area."

"Oh, my gosh," Wally said. "I had a feeling you were Santa all the time ... but—"

"That's all right, Wally," Santa said kindly. "I understand."

After they picked up the luggage at the hotel, they headed out to Fort Lincoln, five miles south of Mandan. Wally drove the car up to the top of a big hill where there were three blockhouses.

Santa said, "Wally, we can unload everything here, and you can head back to Mandan if you'd like."

Wally was more excited now than confused. "Uh, n-no," he said. "I'd like to wait around with you if you don't mind. This is even more exciting than watching the Green Bay Packers playing at Lambeau Field!"

A minute later, the sleigh and reindeer approached from the south with Ethan and Patrick waving to everyone on the ground. Soon, the sleigh came in for a smooth landing twenty yards away as Wally watched in total wonder.

As they were flying back to the North Pole, Willzer asked, "How did the Frosty testing go today?"

Patrick answered, "I think we freaked out a bunch of alligators in Florida, but the testing went very well. Frosty overheated slightly toward the end, but everything else tested out perfectly. I think we're actually ready for tomorrow."

"Ho! Ho! Ho! Frosty's ready to go!" said Santa.

"Wow!" Olivia added. "Everyone in the world's going to get some snow this Christmas."

Willzer said, "You and the rest of the scientists working on this project have done excellent work, Patrick."

Patrick beamed.

8

Christmas Eve had finally arrived! There was a flurry of activity going on at the North Pole, most of it focused on getting Santa's sleigh and reindeer ready for their important journey.

The elves looked a little like worker bees as they swarmed over Santa's sleigh—loading it and checking and double-checking every other detail for the long flight. Other elves were pampering the reindeer, making sure they were well-fed and groomed for the strenuous day ahead.

Patrick and his fellow scientists were making a few last minute adjustments on Frosty. When they'd finished, each of the scientist elves gave Frosty a gentle pat or two for good luck.

Patrick was smiling the whole time. He was not only proud of all the work they'd done on Frosty in just a few days, but he was also fired up because Santa was letting him ride on the sleigh to monitor Frosty this Christmas Eve. It was so exciting for Patrick he could hardly stand it.

The reindeer were getting more anxious by the minute. They could hardly wait to get underway.

Dancer mumbled under his breath, "Let's get on with this."

Prancer, who was standing next to Dancer, said, "Santa, enough already. I'm ready to boogie."

Rudolph was a true leader, and he waited more patiently. He knew it was only a matter of seconds before they were on their way, and there was nothing he could do but wait as calmly as possible.

Just as Rudolph had anticipated, less than ten seconds later, Santa gave Mrs. Claus a kiss, then he got on board the sleigh. Patrick, who was already

standing in the back of the sleigh near Frosty, smiled and waved good-bye to everyone.

Santa said, "Ho! Ho! Ho! Let's go, my Christmas Eve reindeer!"—and the reindeer led the sleigh slowly into the air as everyone down below waved and applauded with great glee. Moments later, the sleigh and reindeer accelerated into the sky like a flash.

For Patrick, the next several hours were beyond anything he could ever have imagined. He was the first elf ever to get a chance to witness one of the great miracles of the universe—Santa delivering gifts to all the good boys and girls on planet Earth.

But Patrick was an important part of another incredible miracle that was happening this particular Christmas Eve. Wherever the sleigh flew, Patrick's creation, Frosty, spread ice crystals into the atmosphere—which soon became big, beautiful, soft flakes of falling snow.

When the adults all around the world saw snowflakes falling to the ground, they woke their kids up and showed them what was happening.

Many of those kids were so excited they didn't even notice the presents Santa had put under their Christmas trees. They ran right past them on the way outside to play in the snow.

The snow that Frosty was producing was perfect for making snowballs and snowmen and snow forts. The world was rapidly becoming a winter wonderland of snow, and everyone was having a blast playing in it.

After visiting almost the entire planet, Santa, Patrick, and the reindeer came down the homestretch. Only the mainland of the United States and the country of Canada were left before they would return to the North Pole.

As they flew over the United States, Santa urged Patrick to have Frosty spread a few extra crystals over some of the towns with Santa's favorite names. Santa Claus, Arizona, got an extra sprinkling—as did Santa Claus, Indiana, and Santa, Idaho. Christmas, Florida, and Noel, Missouri, got an extra coating of snow crystals, too.

Yes, the world was having one of the best Christmases *ever*, thanks largely to Frosty, who

was working flawlessly. With just a few million stops left to go, Santa's sleigh approached the Hooooshkas' house north of Mandan.

Despite the fact that it was very late on Christmas Eve and barely above zero, the Hooooshka triplets were standing outside, waiting eagerly for Santa. As soon as the Hooooshkas spotted the sleigh and reindeer approaching them, still more than a mile away, they waved and yelled and jumped up and down!

When the sleigh finally came in for a landing in their yard, the Hooooshka triplets were so excited they didn't know what to do. Tyler ran over and started petting and hugging each of the reindeer. Braydon headed directly for Santa and gave him a big hug. Brian ran over to see Patrick and Frosty. The Hooooshka triplets were truly having the time of their lives ... but soon it got even better.

"Come on aboard, boys!" Santa said. "I brought you each a little something."

Santa and Patrick helped the Hooooshka triplets on board. Then Santa reached into his red

bag and said, "Here, boys. I have a feeling this is what you wanted for Christmas."

Santa handed each of them a roll of rope and a new cowboy hat—just like the real cowboys have. The Hooooshka triplets loved their gifts. Right away, they put on their new hats and started knotting their ropes so they could lasso something later.

"Santa, thanks so much," Tyler said excitedly.

"Yeah, Santa," Braydon added cheerfully. "I don't think I deserve this, but you're the best!"

"This is all *so* cool!" Brian exclaimed with a huge smile.

Santa said, "All three of you are so welcome. I can't thank you boys enough for showing everyone in your class what Christmas spirit is all about. I have a feeling you three will hold Christmas dear to your hearts forever."

After that, Santa offered the Hooooshka triplets an opportunity of the ages! "Would you boys like to stay on board with Patrick and me?" Santa asked. "I'll let you help deliver gifts to the rest of the fourth graders in your class if you'd like to."

"Right now!?" Braydon hollered, jumping up and down.

"We can fly with you!?" Brian asked, so excited he could hardly stand it.

Tyler was so fired up, he was speechless. He just stood there with his mouth wide open.

Eventually, Santa got the Hooooshka triplets to calm down and buckle up in the seats next to him. "Hold on to your new cowboy hats, boys!" Santa cried as they lifted off. "We're headed for Mandan!"

How great was this! The Hooooshka triplets were flying for the first time in their lives—and they were flying with Santa and his reindeer on Christmas Eve! Frosty was spreading snow crystals all over the area, and the crystals were soon becoming the most beautiful, huge snowflakes.

The Hooooshkas suddenly got real quiet, in total wonderment of what they were seeing. They flew over Interstate 94, then over the Mandan Refinery which was lit up for Christmas with millions of multicolored lights. From there, they headed southwest and flew over Mandan's Main

Street, then slowly turned northwest and approached Abby Lu's house.

Abby Lu was outside waiting with her dad. As the sleigh got within a hundred yards of the house and closed in, her dad's eyes got bigger and bigger as the sleigh got closer and closer.

"I told you, Dad! I told you!" Abby Lu yelled, as she grabbed her dad and shook him.

Abby Lu's dad stared skyward in total disbelief and watched as the reindeer drawn sleigh landed on their roof with Santa and the Hooooshkas and an elf on board. "I'm so sorry, Abby Lu. I'll never doubt you again," he managed to whisper to his daughter. He cleared his throat and called up to Santa, "When Abby Lu told me she had you and some elves as substitute teachers—and she needed to be awake to see you tonight—I thought she'd gone a little wacko."

"Ho! Ho! Ho, Mr. Kramer!" Santa shouted from the roof. "I understand. Uh ... when we're finished at your house, would you mind if Abby Lu joins us for a short ride? We're going to pick up all her classmates eventually and go for a short ride. I can have Abby Lu back here in about forty-five minutes."

Abby Lu's dad saw the look in his daughter's eyes, and there was no way he could say no. Actually, he wished he could go along with them.

After Santa's work was finished at the Kramer house and Abby Lu was safely on board, their next destination was Lefty Faris's house. As they approached it, Lefty was looking out his second story bedroom window, anxiously awaiting Santa's arrival. In another bedroom down the hall, Lefty's parents were sleeping soundly as Rudolph led the reindeer toward the roof.

Lefty couldn't believe it when he saw the sleigh and reindeer, Santa, an elf, Abby Lu, and the Hooooshkas! He opened up his window and cried, "Hi, Santa! Hi, Abby Lu! Hi, Brian, Braydon, and Tyler! Hi, reindeer! Hi, Mr. Elf Guy!"

Lefty's yelling woke his mom and dad up. They quickly ran to Lefty's room to see what was going on—but Lefty had already run downstairs to put his parka on over his pajamas, and he was running outside.

Mr. and Mrs. Faris quickly grabbed their coats, put them on over their pajamas, and ran out the door barefoot into the snow in their front yard. When they looked up and saw who and what was on their roof, they stared for several seconds in total disbelief. Santa called down to them, "Mr. and Mrs. Faris, it was great having Lefty in class the past few days. I wonder—after we leave your gifts here, would you mind if he joins the rest of us for a few minutes? We're going to visit the rest of his classmates and take them all for a little ride. It won't take long."

Mr. and Mrs. Faris still looked like they were in shock. Finally, Mrs. Faris managed to say, "Uh ... sure ... Santa."

A few stops later—after Thomas, Dakota, Holly, and Trace had been picked up—they approached the roof of Tommy Muscatell's house. A small red light on Frosty blinked briefly, but it turned off before Patrick even noticed.

Eventually, all twenty-three of Miss Kemper's students were comfortably crowded on board Santa's sleigh, having a fantastic time circling once above Mandan and Bismarck, as Frosty spread snow crystals everywhere. Santa cried, "Why don't we give Miss Kemper another big Christmas Eve surprise! Let's fly by her room at the Mandan Hospital!"

Everyone cheered—except Tyler Hooooshka, who was standing in back of the sleigh next to Patrick. He noticed Frosty's red light was blinking—and Frosty seemed to be shaking a little.

Tyler tapped Patrick on the shoulder. "Uh, Patrick? Is Frosty supposed to be doing that?"

By the time Patrick turned around to take a look, the shaking had gotten much worse—then Frosty went absolutely **BONKERS!** Instead of harmless snow crystals, Frosty started shooting out massive amounts of pink sparks that fortunately disintegrated into nothingness long before they fell to the ground. Seconds later, as the reindeer and everyone on board the sleigh watched in horror, Frosty shook so hard—he broke loose from the back of the sleigh and started falling down to the town below.

Frosty had fallen about ten feet when he stopped abruptly—and now he was trailing behind the sleigh by a rope. Tyler Hooooshka had lassoed Frosty, but the out of control snowmaking machine was getting away from Tyler fast. Two seconds later, Frosty was flying precariously twenty-five feet behind the sleigh held by one rope—which Tyler was hanging onto for dear life.

Quickly, Tommy, Arly, Holly, Abby Lu, and Dakota grabbed the rope and helped Tyler—but Frosty began winning this tug-of-war in no time at all. He started slipping further away from the sleigh—and Tyler was rapidly running out of rope.

Brian and Braydon rushed to the back of the sleigh as quickly as they could. Braydon threw his rope, but Frosty was a tough target to hit at that distance and he missed. Brian gave it a try, successfully snagging Frosty on his first attempt, and several more fourth graders grabbed Brian's rope. They pulled with every bit of strength they had.

On his second try, Braydon lassoed Frosty, too—so Frosty was now held by three ropes. Twenty-three students and Patrick were holding on with all the strength they could muster as a trail of pink sparks continued to shoot out of Frosty, who suddenly started shaking more violently than ever. If something didn't happen soon, Frosty was going to burn the ropes or break them—and then he'd fall down on the town below.

Santa looked back frantically and yelled, **"Patrick, what do you want me to do!?"**

"Just keep flying!" Patrick exclaimed, horrified, but trying to figure out some solution.

About this time, Tiny's wife came into their garage where Tiny was just finishing the job of putting new chrome wheels on his monster pickup truck. The wheels had been a Christmas gift from his wife and two kids.

"Tiny, grab your binoculars and come outside!" she said, with a look of panic in her eyes.

Tiny quickly grabbed his binoculars from his glove compartment and followed his wife outside.

"Look!" she cried, pointing up into the sky.

"Oh, my gosh!" Tiny boomed. **"It's Santa and Miss Kemper's class—and they're in big trouble!"** Tiny ran into his garage, got in his pickup, and took off—following the sleigh—as it flew northwest above Mandan.

Suddenly, Frosty started shooting out big glowing red and green sparks shaped like snowflakes, which fortunately burned out before any of them hit the ground. The growing crowd now watching from down below looked up and saw the most unbelievable sight imaginable. It was like some strange Fourth of July Christmas comet flying above them. The people of Mandan and Bismarck were seeing a super-exciting spectacle that no one would ever forget.

Miss Kemper was sleeping soundly in her hospital room as this was going on, but she was soon awakened by nurse Carla. Carla helped Miss Kemper over to the window. They watched together apprehensively as something flew in their direction, but it was too far away at this point to really tell what it was.

9

It was late on Christmas night. The Hooooshka triplets were sound asleep, scattered around on the living room furniture, their new cowboy hats nearby. They'd all collapsed a few hours earlier, totally exhausted after enjoying the greatest Christmas Eve and Christmas Day imaginable.

An old pickup truck drove into the Hooooshkas' yard. A tall, slim, unshaven, dark-haired man grabbed something from the cab of the truck, got out, then walked over to the passenger side and opened the door. A pretty lady with long brown hair got out of the truck. The man and woman held each other closely as they walked to the front door of the house and knocked softly.

Tyler Hooooshka woke up a bit, stumbled to the front door, and opened it up. "Mom! Daddy!" he said, surprised to see his parents. "Are you back to visit us? … Hey, where did you get those new rolls of rope, Daddy?"

Before Mr. Hooooshka could answer that question, Brian and Braydon were awakened by Tyler's voice. They ran over to join Tyler and their mom and dad by the front door.

The Hooooshka triplets hugged their parents, then Mr. Hooooshka handed each of his boys a new roll of rope.

"Boys," Mr. Hooooshka said with tears in his eyes, "your mother and I are here to stay—if you'll have us."

Mrs. Hooooshka was crying. "And we're gonna be good parents to you boys for the first time in our lives," she said.

Brian asked, "What made you decide that now, Mom and Daddy?"

ABOUT THE AUTHOR

 Kevin Kremer loves Christmas. Many of his favorite memories involve Christmases while he was growing up in Mandan, North Dakota. His first book, *A Kremer Christmas Miracle*, contains many of those memories.

Kremer has never met a Pittsburgh Steelers fan he didn't like. He enjoys writing books almost as much as watching the Steelers win Super Bowls.

Dr. Kremer has now started a writing/publishing company to help people with any aspect of their own book projects. To contact him regarding writing or publishing projects you need help with, school author visitations, or to purchase books, go to:

web site: www.snowinsarasota.com
e-mail: snowinsarasota@aol.com